For **Shabo**, my imaginary playmate,
and for **Ross**, **Mimi** and **Vera**, my real ones —B. L.

For **Mom** and **Dad** —A. S.

Book design by Sara Gillingham.
Typeset in Coffeedance.
The illustrations in this book were rendered in oil and gesso on paper.
Manufactured in China.

Library of Congress Cataloging-in-Publication Data
Levin, Bridget.
Rules of the wild : an unruly book of manners / by Bridget Levin : illustrated by Amanda Shepherd.
p. cm.
Summary: Rhyming text explores how proper behavior for young animals is
different from what is expected of young children.
ISBN 0-8118-4226-6
[1. Behavior—Fiction. 2. Animals—Fiction. 3. Stories in rhyme.] I. Shepherd, Amanda, ill. II. Title.
PZ8.3.L575Ru 2004
[E]—dc22
2003017343

Distributed in Canada by Raincoast Books
9050 Shaughnessy Street, Vancouver, British Columbia V6P 6E5

10 9 8 7 6 5 4 3 2 1

Chronicle Books LLC
85 Second Street, San Francisco, California 94105
www.chroniclekids.com

Rules of the Wild

An Unruly Book of Manners

written by Bridget Levin
illustrated by Amanda Shepherd

chronicle books · san francisco

If your mom had a tail
or your father a mane,
the rules of your house
might not be such a pain.

Mother Piggy would say,
"Eat whatever you like."

Father Fruit Bat declare,

"You can stay up all night."

Mother Dolphin would nod,
"Splashing is fine."

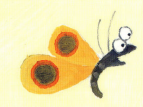

Father Lion exclaim,
"That roar sounds divine!"

If your mom was cold-blooded,
your dad tended to drool,
Could you mind all your manners?
Would you follow the rules?

Mother Snake wouldn't scold,
"Don't leave clothes on the floor."

Father Camel wouldn't huff,
"Please don't spit any more!"

Mother Groundhog would say,
"Sure, go play in the dirt."

Father Elephant declare,
"On your mark, get set...
SQUIRT!"

If your parents were four-legged
or had wings, tails or tusks,
would you know all the mustn'ts?
Would you know all the musts?

Mother Cow wouldn't urge,
"Chew with your mouth closed, my dear."

Father Walrus wouldn't fuss,
"We don't burp around here."

RIP!

Mother Grizzly would yawn,
"Sure, sleep all winter long."

Father Raccoon would say,
"Fine, dunking food isn't wrong."

But if your father wears clothing
and your mother does, too,
you know how to behave.
you know just what to do.

Don't you?

Are you allowed to

	Elephant	Cow	Walrus	Wolf	Butterfly	Pig
eat whatever you want?	yes	yes	yes	YES!	yes	YES!!!
stay up all night?	NO	NO	NO	yes!	NO	NO
spit?	yes	NO	yes	NO	NO!	NO
splash each other?	YES!	NO!	yes!	yes	NO	NO
make loud noises?	YES!!!	yes	YES!	yes	NO	YES!
bathe in the dirt?	yes	NO	NO	NO	NO	YES!
chew with your mouth open?	yes	YES! YES! YES!	NO	yes	NO	yes
burp out loud?	yes	yes	yes	NO	NO!	NO
dunk food in your drink?	yes	NO	yes	YES!!!	NO	yes

yes	yes	yes	yes	yesssss	yes	NO!
YES!!	NO	yes	NO	yes	NO	NO!
NO	yes	NO	YES!	yes	NO!	NO!
NO!	YES!!	NO!	NO	NO	NO	NO!
NO	yes	YES!!!!!	yes	NO	NO	NO!
NO	NO!	yes	yes	NO	YES!!!	NO!
NO	NO	yes	YES!	NO	yes	NO!
NO	NO	NO	NO	NO	NO	NO!
NO	yes	NO	NO	NO	NO	NO!